PRINCE FLY GUY

Tedd Arnold

Cartwheel Books
An Imprint of Scholastic Inc.

For Prince Garrett
and Prince Caleb

Library of Congress Cataloging-in-Publication Data

Arnold, Tedd, author.
Prince Fly Guy / Tedd Arnold.
pages cm. — (Fly Guy ; 15)
Summary: Buzz is writing a fairy tale for homework, and Fly Guy naturally assumes the role of a handsome prince, who fends off a giant and rescues a beautiful princess.
ISBN 978-0-545-66275-8
1. Flies—Juvenile fiction. 2. Imagination—Juvenile fiction. 3. Homework—Juvenile fiction. [1. Flies—Fiction. 2. Imagination—Fiction. 3. Fairy tales—Fiction. 4. Humorous stories.] I. Title. II. Series: Arnold, Tedd. Fly Guy ; 15.

PZ7.A7379Pr 2015
813.54—dc23
[E]

2015000212

10 9 8 7 6 5 4 3 2 1   15 16 17 18 19

Printed in China   38
First printing, September 2015
Book design by Steve Ponzo

A boy had a pet fly.
He named him Fly Guy.
And Fly Guy could
say the boy's name –

Chapter 1

One night, Buzz said,
"I have homework to do.
I have to write a fairy tale.
Can you help me, Fly Guy?"

"Well," said Buzz,
"how does this sound?
Once upon a time..."

YEZZ

"Okay," said Buzz.
"Once upon a time,
there was an ugly troll."

"You don't like that?
Well, what about a
smelly pig herder?"

"No? What about a
handsome prince?"

"Okay," said Buzz.
"The handsome prince
walked to the dark castle."

"Maybe instead of walking," said Buzz, "what if he *rode* to the dark castle?"

"No! I've got it! He *flew* to the dark castle?"

Chapter 2

"At the dark castle," said Buzz, "the handsome prince ate cold porridge."

"What if he kissed a frog?"

"I've got it! He rescued a beautiful princess."

Chapter 3

"The giant chased the handsome prince and the beautiful princess."

"He knocked them down
to the ground."

"The princess threw her crown."

"It hit the giant on the nose."

"The giant fell down."

"He ran away."

"The prince and the
princess flew home."

"They made matching crowns."

"And they lived

"The end," said Buzz.

"I like my fairy tale," said Buzz.
"Hey, want to write another one?"

"Okay. Once there was a hairy dwarf . . ."